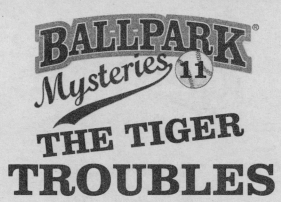

BALLPARK Mysteries 11
THE TIGER
TROUBLES

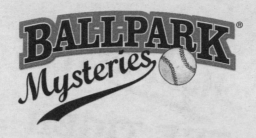

BALLPARK Mysteries

Also by David A. Kelly

Babe Ruth and the Baseball Curse

BALLPARK® Mysteries 11

THE TIGER TROUBLES

by David A. Kelly

illustrated by Mark Meyers

A STEPPING STONE BOOK™
Random House 🏠 New York

This book is dedicated to Mo'ne Davis, a Little League pitcher from Philadelphia, who was the first girl to win a Little League World Series game as well as the first girl to pitch a shutout in the Little League World Series! Mo'ne is Kate's new hero, because she reminds the world that baseball isn't just for boys. —D.A.K.

To Phil—thanks for the help on so many projects! —M.M.

"Baseball is a ballet without music." —Ernie Harwell, longtime Detroit Tigers broadcaster

Text copyright © 2015 by David A. Kelly
Cover art and interior illustrations copyright © 2015 by Mark Meyers

All rights reserved. Published in the United States by Random House Children's Books, a division of Random House LLC, a Penguin Random House Company, New York.

Random House and the colophon are registered trademarks and A Stepping Stone Book and the colophon are trademarks of Random House LLC. Ballpark Mysteries® is a registered trademark of Upside Research, Inc.

Visit us on the Web!
SteppingStonesBooks.com
randomhousekids.com
Educators and librarians, for a variety of teaching tools, visit us at
RHTeachersLibrarians.com

Library of Congress Cataloging-in-Publication Data
Kelly, David A.
The Tiger troubles / by David A. Kelly ; illustrated by Mark Meyers.
p. cm. — (Ballpark mysteries ; 11)
"A Stepping Stone Book."
Summary: "When Mike and Kate visit Detroit, someone is blackmailing the Tigers' famous slugger, Tony Maloney." — Provided by publisher.
ISBN 978-0-385-37878-9 (pbk.) — ISBN 978-0-385-37879-6 (lib. bdg.) —
ISBN 978-0-385-37880-2 (ebook)
[1. Baseball—Fiction. 2. Detroit Tigers (Baseball team)—Fiction. 3. Extortion—Fiction. 4. Cousins—Fiction. 5. Detroit (Mich.)—Fiction. 6. Mystery and detective stories.]
I. Meyers, Mark, illustrator. II. Title.
PZ7.K2936Tig 2015   [Fic]—dc23   2014011734

Printed in the United States of America
10 9 8 7 6 5

This book has been officially leveled by using the
F&P Text Level Gradient™ Leveling System.

Random House Children's Books supports the First Amendment
and celebrates the right to read.

Contents

The Missing Tiger

Kate Hopkins slipped into the driver's seat of a shiny red convertible. She pressed the center of the steering wheel twice.

Beep! Beep!

A group of Detroit Tigers baseball players stood on the grass in front of the car. The players jumped at the sound of the horn. One of them dropped his glove. When they turned around and saw Kate at the wheel, they laughed and waved.

"Hey, it's my turn to drive!" said Kate's

cousin Mike Walsh. He was sitting in the passenger seat.

Mike and Kate were visiting Detroit with Kate's dad. Mr. Hopkins was a baseball scout for the Los Angeles Dodgers. Sometimes he took Kate and Mike with him on his trips. This time they were going to see a Tigers baseball game. But before the game, he had arranged for them to ride in a classic car parade.

"I don't think *either* of you should be driving," Mr. Hopkins said. He opened the driver's-side door and motioned for them to climb out. "We should be looking for my friend Tony."

Mike pulled a baseball card out of his pocket. It showed a tall African American baseball player wearing a white uniform with a big blue *D* on the front. Across the bottom of the card in gold letters was the name Tony "The Tiger" Maloney. "I hope he'll give me his autograph," Mike said. "I told my friends at school I'd get it."

Mr. Hopkins shook his head. "I'm not sure he will," he said. "He injured his wrist earlier in the season. Tony told me his coach made him promise to protect his wrist and not sign any autographs until after the season."

Tony was the new star outfielder for the Detroit Tigers. He and Mr. Hopkins were old friends, and Tony had invited the three of them to meet him at the Detroit Car Cruise on Woodward Avenue and ride in the parade with him. The Car Cruise was the largest car meet anywhere. People from around the world brought their old, special, or customized cars to show them off.

Mike, Kate, and Mr. Hopkins walked down the line of parked cars, looking for Tony. Each car they passed was crazier than the last. There

was a bright green hot rod with a horn that made an *aaaaoooggaaa* sound and a shiny blue pickup truck that shot flames out of its exhaust pipes! There was even an old-fashioned brown and yellow car with a big, shaggy dog sitting in its rumble seat. Kate and Mike tried barking at the dog but couldn't get him to bark back.

"There sure are a lot of cars here," Mike said.

"That's why Detroit's called the Motor City," Kate said. "I read it's where all the big car companies started. Like Henry Ford, with his Model T. It was the first really popular car. They didn't cost too much, and Ford figured out how to make lots of them fast." Kate loved to read. Whenever Mike and Kate went to a new place, Kate would read up on it.

Mike, Kate, and Mr. Hopkins walked up and down the lines of parked cars until they came to a white convertible from the 1950s. The top was down, and the inside was bright red leather.

When he saw it, Mr. Hopkins let out a low whistle. "Boy, they sure don't make them like this anymore. It's a 1959 Cadillac."

The car was long and flat, except for two big fins that rose up on either side of the trunk. The fins had red lights in them that made them look like the tail of a rocket.

Nearby, the other Detroit Tigers players were climbing into different classic cars for the parade. Mr. Hopkins checked his watch. "Tony told me to meet him here," he said. "We're going to miss the parade unless we find him!"

Mr. Hopkins waved his hand. "Come on, follow me," he said. The three ran over to the last car in line. It hadn't started yet. Two Tigers players were sitting in the backseat.

"Excuse me," Mr. Hopkins said to the player closest to him. "We were supposed to meet Tony the Tiger for the parade, but he's not here. Do you know where he is?"

"He's gone?" the player asked. "He was over there earlier, but someone left a note for him in the car. I don't know what it said, but it sure spooked him. Once he read it, he took off like a flash!"

The line of cars filled with Detroit Tigers players pulled away.

"Something must be wrong," Mr. Hopkins said. "I can't believe Tony would have left without telling us."

"Maybe it was an emergency," Kate said.

"Could be," Mr. Hopkins said. "I'll try to call him to see what's going on. Why don't you head back to the car, in case he shows up?"

Mike and Kate walked back to the white convertible.

Mike scuffed the dirt with his sneaker. "Rats! Just look how cool this car is." He leaned over the door and peered inside. That was when he noticed something stuck between the seat and the driver's-side door. He reached down and fished around. When his hand emerged, he was holding a piece of notebook paper. Mike unfolded it and read it. His eyes grew wide.

"Kate, you've got to see this!" he said. He held it out for her.

LEAVE MORE OF YOU-KNOW-WHAT IN THE
USUAL PLACE BEFORE TODAY'S GAME—

OR IT WILL BE THREE STRIKES FOR YOUR

SPECIAL TROPHY!

"Wow! I bet this is what made Tony take off," Kate said. "Somebody's blackmailing him!"

Mike studied the note. "What do you think 'you-know-what' means?" he asked.

"I don't know," Kate said. "But that trophy sounds important." She tucked the note into her pocket. She and Mike searched the car for more clues. When Mr. Hopkins returned a few minutes later, they hadn't found anything new.

"Tony didn't answer my call, but he might be back at the stadium getting ready for today's game," Mr. Hopkins said. "I guess you didn't find him over here."

"Nope," said Kate. "But we did find this." She took the note out of her pocket and handed

it to her father. "Someone's threatening Tony!"

Mr. Hopkins shook his head as he read the note. "This isn't good," he said. "We've got to head to the stadium right away!"

A Shower of Baseballs

Thirty minutes later, Mr. Hopkins pulled their car into a parking lot across from the stadium. Mr. Hopkins paid the attendant and led Mike and Kate toward the main entrance.

"Wow! This is amazing," Mike said as they got closer.

Tiger heads were mounted on the stadium's outside walls, and sculptures of tigers prowled along the rooftops. There were tigers everywhere!

On the brick plaza in front of the stadium, a huge tan tiger sat on its haunches. Its tail curled around it. The tiger looked as tall as a house! One of its giant paws towered high in the air, ready to take a swipe at rival teams. The tiger's mouth hung open, baring its large fangs.

"*¡Qué tigre tan grande!*" Kate said. "What a big tiger!"

"*¡Tienes razón!*" her dad said. "You're right!" Mr. Hopkins spoke Spanish since he worked with a lot of baseball players from other countries. Kate liked to practice with him.

"I know that tigers are the largest species of cat, but that's a *really big* cat!" Kate said.

Mike ran over to the statue and stood underneath the tiger's outstretched paw.

Kate scampered after him. "Can you take our picture?" she asked her dad. She took off her blue L.A. Dodgers baseball cap so the funny face she was making would show more.

"Sure," Mr. Hopkins said. He pulled out his phone. Mike put his arm around Kate, like he was scared. They both looked up with wide eyes and raised their arms above their heads, pretending to shield themselves from the tiger's attacking paw.

Click. Click. Click. Mr. Hopkins snapped away. When he was done, he laughed. "This is great. It looks like you're being attacked by a giant tiger!"

"This place feels more like a jungle than a ballpark!" Kate said.

"Well, maybe it's time to *chase* a tiger," Mr. Hopkins said. "Let's go around to the other gate and see if we can find Tony."

Mike and Kate trailed along behind Mr. Hopkins as they headed down the sidewalk to the employee gate at the other corner. Two

more huge tigers prowled over the top of this entrance.

Mike, Kate, and Mr. Hopkins walked up to the employee checking identification. Mr. Hopkins showed his special L.A. Dodgers pass, and the security guard let him pass.

Kate was just about to push through the gate when an orange and white blur streaked by the side of her head.

"Watch out, Kate!" Mike called from behind her. "There's a tiger loose!"

Before Kate could move, a paw swiped at her head. The paw hit the brim of her baseball hat and knocked it flying. It landed with a plunk on the ground.

Kate ducked and covered her head.

But Mike started laughing. He picked up Kate's hat and handed it back to her. Then he pointed to a small ledge above the entrance.

Kate looked up and started laughing, too.

Perched on the edge was a large orange and white tabby cat. It stared back at Kate and Mike, then lost interest and started licking its right paw.

Kate stomped her foot and swiped at Mike with her hat. "I thought that was a tiger's paw!" she said.

"Well, a tiger is a cat," Mike said. "A *big* cat." He reached up on his tiptoes and scratched the cat's side. It started purring.

"I see you met Tabby," said a voice behind them. A teenage girl walked around Kate and Mike, toward the gate. She wore a blue and white Tigers T-shirt. A security tag hung from her neck. Dark curly hair poked out from under her Tigers baseball cap.

"Hi, Jane," the security guard said. "It's going to be a great game today."

"Sure is," Jane replied. Then she pointed up at the cat and said to Kate and Mike, "Tabby's a city cat that likes to hang around the stadium and watch the games. Sometimes fans bring her food. She usually leaves people alone, but

18

maybe she didn't like your L.A. Dodgers hat."

"I guess she's a real Tigers fan," Kate's dad said.

Jane laughed. "I think so," she said. Then they pushed through the security gate one at a time. "Enjoy the game!" Jane said as she headed off to work.

Mike, Kate, and Mr. Hopkins headed for the Tigers' clubhouse to look for Tony. Halfway down the main walkway, Kate gave her dad's shirt a tug. She pointed through an archway to a food court area. In the middle of it was a merry-go-round.

"Can Mike and I go check it out?" she asked.

"Sure," Mr. Hopkins said. "When you're done, just follow this walkway and meet me at the Tigers' locker room."

"Yippee!" said Mike. He and Kate ran to the merry-go-round. It looked just like one at a fair

or amusement park, except all the animals on it were tigers!

Mike was just about to see if they could get on the ride when Kate called out and pointed across the food court.

"Look! There's Tony the Tiger!" she said.

Mike followed Kate's finger. Tony was on the other side of the merry-go-round. Even though he was walking away from them, he looked just like the picture on his baseball card.

"What's he carrying?" Kate asked.

Mike frowned and scratched his head. "I

don't know. But it looks a little like a tiger!"

Mike was right. Tony was carrying a stuffed toy tiger under his arm. He seemed to be headed for the back of the food court. When Tony reached it, he set the stuffed tiger down between a tall brick pillar and the wall and then quickly walked toward the locker room without looking back.

"That was weird," Mike said.

"I know," Kate said. "Let's go take a look."

They rushed over to examine the stuffed animal. Kate reached behind the pillar and picked it up.

"Ah, this doesn't feel like any stuffed tiger that *I'd* like to play with." She handed the tiger to Mike.

"It's lumpy!" Mike said. "And heavy!" He lifted it up over his head to get a look underneath it. "What's in here?"

But as he peeked beneath the tiger, there was a sudden *zzzip*.

Five baseballs fell out of the bottom of the tiger.

Bonk! Bonk! Bonk! Bonk! Bonk!

One after another, the baseballs hit Mike in the head!

Tony's Problem

"Ouch!" Mike said. "Ouch! Ouch! Ouch! Ouch!"

The balls dropped to the floor at Mike's feet. As he rubbed his head, Kate scrambled to pick them up. Instead of being red and white like normal baseballs, they were black and orange tiger-print leather.

"Are you okay?" Kate asked Mike when she stood up.

Mike stopped rubbing his head. "Yeah," he said with a smile. "It takes more than a few baseballs to stop me."

"I know," Kate said. "Usually it takes a few chocolate chip cookies."

"Hey, I call those energy disks," Mike said. "They give me the power I need to play baseball."

Kate rolled her eyes. She held up the tiger baseballs. "I don't think you'll be playing with these," she said. "Look, they're all signed by Tony the Tiger!"

Tony had signed his name with a bright gold marker across the sweet spot of each ball.

"These must be the 'you-know-what' mentioned in the note!" Mike said. "Someone's stolen Tony's trophy, and they're making him sign baseballs! He's being blackmailed!"

The sound of scraping metal from around the corner startled Mike and Kate. Nearby, ballpark workers had just started to open up their food stands for the game.

"We've got to put the tiger back and get out of here before we're caught," Kate said. "Then we can figure out what to do."

Mike turned the tiger over and noticed a zipper on its bottom. It had unzipped when he had picked up the tiger. Mike and Kate stuffed the signed baseballs back into the tiger and zipped the hole closed. Then they placed the tiger on the ground behind the pillar where they had found it.

"Maybe it's some kind of baseball prank," Kate said as they headed to the Tigers' locker room. "I've read how players like to pull pranks on rookies and new players. Maybe they're making Tony do funny things because he's new."

"I don't know," Mike said. "That note in the car seemed pretty serious. 'Three strikes' doesn't seem like a joke."

Mr. Hopkins was waiting for them outside

the locker room. "There you are," he said. "I
was just going to come looking for you. Tony's
in here." Mr. Hopkins led them into the locker
room. The wide wooden lockers stood along
the outside walls, with a black chair in front

of each one. The room was filled with baseball players as well as press and other media people. Mr. Hopkins, Kate, and Mike made their way over to Tony's locker. The sign above it read TONY MALONEY.

Tony looked just like his picture on Mike's baseball card. He was tall, with frizzy hair, and was wearing his Tigers uniform. He had a black baseball glove on his left hand. With his right hand, he was snapping a baseball into the glove. *Pop! Pop! Pop!*

"So you're Mike and Kate," he said. "Nice to meet you. I'm Tony Maloney. But everyone calls me Tony the Tiger."

Mike smiled. "We know." He pulled Tony's baseball card out of his pocket and held it up. "It says that on your baseball card. Could you sign it for me?"

Tony stopped throwing the baseball and

glanced at the older man standing next to him. He was also wearing a Tigers uniform. "I'm afraid you need to ask my coach about that," he said, nodding at the man.

The coach shook his head. "Tony injured his wrist. I told him he's got to save his hand for baseball," he said. "No more autographs until after the season. Sorry, kids!"

The coach patted Tony on the shoulder and started toward the dugout. "See you on the field, Tony," he said. "Go, Tigers! We're going to eat 'em up today!"

Mike lowered the card. "But we just saw—" Kate elbowed him in the side. Mike cleared his throat. "Um, we just saw some really cool cars at the car show," he said. He slipped the baseball card back into his pocket.

"Oh yeah," Tony said. "Sorry. I know we were supposed to meet there, but I had to leave early. Something came up, and I had to get back here in a hurry."

Mike and Kate exchanged glances.

Kate pulled out the letter they had found in the car. "We know. We found this note in the front seat." She held the note up.

Tony took the piece of paper. He removed his baseball cap and ran his fingers through his hair. "I must have dropped this when I left," he said.

"It looks like someone's giving you trouble," Kate said.

Mr. Hopkins held his hand up. "Kate, hold on a minute," he said.

But Kate continued. "Is that why we saw you hide a stuffed tiger?" she asked.

Tony dropped his hat. He looked confused. "What do you mean?" he asked. He let his hand with the glove fall to his side.

Mike stepped forward. "We saw you carrying a stuffed tiger a little while ago," he said.
"You put it down behind the pillar. We picked it
up to take a look at it and found a whole bunch
of signed baseballs!"

Tony's eyes opened wide. "Did you put
it back?" he asked. "Please tell me you put it
back."

Kate nodded. "We put it back just the way
we found it. Then we came to talk to you," she
said. "To find out what's going on."

Tony hung his head. "I'll tell you what's
going on," he said. "I've got big problems."

Chasing a Tiger

"Someone's blackmailing me," Tony said.

"You mean that someone's threatening you?" Mr. Hopkins asked. "What do they want?"

Tony leaned against his locker. "They want signed baseballs and other stuff," he said. "I don't know who it is. The only person I can think of who might be doing it is Roger, our pitcher." Tony pointed to a tall redheaded baseball player. "He's famous for playing practical jokes on new players. But he's been nice to me as far as I know."

"What if you stop signing things?" Mr. Hopkins asked.

Tony shook his head. "Whoever is sending the notes has a trophy of mine. If I don't do what the notes tell me to, I'll never get it back."

"Wow," Mike said. "Like a World Series trophy?"

Tony laughed. "No," he said. "It's a little silly, but it's my Little League MVP trophy. It's really important to me. I got it when I was twelve. It's always brought me good luck. I want the trophy back, but I don't want anyone on the team to know about it because it's kind of personal."

Tony pulled out his phone. He tapped it with his finger a few times. A picture of a gold trophy popped up on the screen. "That's it," he said.

"How did the thief get the trophy?" Kate asked.

Tony shrugged. "I don't know," he said. "I've been missing it for three weeks. I usually kept it in a safe place, but they were redoing the locker room, so I put the trophy in my bag. After that, I went to a meeting. When I got home, it wasn't in my bag! A couple days after I lost it, I started getting threatening notes. The notes told me to drop off signed baseballs and

T-shirts at different places around the stadium. That's why I left the car show early. I needed to drop off more signed baseballs."

Tony explained that each time he left the stuffed tiger, it came back empty. Usually, he'd find it in a blue Tigers shopping bag outside the locker room.

"Whoever has it must be making lots of money selling my signed stuff. I'm not supposed to autograph things, so they're worth a lot of money," Tony said. "But I'm going to do whatever it takes to get my trophy back."

Kate stepped forward. "What if you just hide somewhere and wait to see who picks up the tiger?" she asked. "Then you'd be able to catch them."

Tony popped a baseball into his glove. "Good idea," he said. "But one of the first notes told me not to go to the police or try to watch. If I do, I'll never see the trophy again. And I can't tell any-one else about this, because I'll get in trouble if Coach knows I'm signing autographs."

"Can you show us the rest of the notes, since we already know?" Kate asked. "Mike and I are pretty good at solving mysteries."

Tony nodded. "Sure thing." He rummaged through his locker and pulled down a pile of papers from the top shelf. "Here they are," he said. He handed them to Kate and then checked his watch. "I'm afraid I've got to get ready for the game now. Let me know if you figure any-thing out."

Mike, Kate, and Mr. Hopkins left the locker room and headed to their seats. They were near the Tigers' dugout on the third-base line. Since it was close to game time, the seats around them were starting to fill up with fans.

Mr. Hopkins sat down. He pulled out a

notebook that he used to keep track of baseball players. Whenever he went to a baseball game, he took lots of notes for work. Sometimes, Kate even helped him by pointing out certain players or helping him grade how well a player hit or fielded.

Mike reclined in the chair and swung his feet back and forth. "These seats are great!" he said. "I really like this ballpark!"

When the Detroit Tigers ran out to the field a short time later, Mike and Kate stood up and cheered. The first New York Mets batter walked up to the plate.

As they sat back down, Kate nudged Mike and pointed toward the pitcher's mound. "There's Roger, the player who Tony suspected," she said. "Let's keep an eye on him."

"As long as we can watch Tony, too," Mike said. "I hear he's a great outfielder!"

From their seats, Mike and Kate had a good view of Tony in center field. Detroit got off to a good start when Roger struck out the first two Mets batters. But when the third Mets batter connected with a fastball, Tony took off running like a shot. He dashed back toward the outfield wall as the ball flew high over second base. It looked like an easy home run. The batter rounded the bases on his way to home.

But Tony didn't give up. He raced to the wall and leapt up just as the ball was flying over the fence. His arm dropped down behind the fence, and the crowd let out a big "Oh no!" But then Tony pulled his arm back up in the air and waved the glove around. Clenched in its webbing was the baseball. He had caught the ball and made the out!

The fans went wild. A woman next to Kate and Mike whistled loudly while other fans

cheered and waved their Tigers baseball caps.

"Woo-hoo! Way to go! Nice catch!" Mike yelled. "Go get 'em, Tigers!" He stamped his feet and clapped a few times and then sat down.

"That's it," Kate said. She pulled out the stack of papers from Tony. "Tony made a catch. Now we need to make a catch. Let's look through these notes that Tony gave us for clues."

Some notes were on plain pieces of notebook paper. Others looked like they had come from a Tigers program, since there were facts about the team on the back. Mike and Kate spent two innings looking at the notes but came up empty.

"Well, that's a dead end," Kate said. "Those notes don't tell us anything."

Mike stared at the last note. There was a cartoon tiger printed in the bottom right corner. He tapped the tiger on the nose and stood up. "That's it!" he said. "The notes can't lead us to the blackmailer, but maybe something else can. We need to go search."

"What?" Kate asked. "What are we going to look for? There's no trail to follow."

Mike smiled. "We're not looking for a trail, Kate. We're looking for a *tail*! A stuffed tiger's tail. Come on, we're going tiger hunting!"

Too Many Pandas

Mike bounded up the aisle toward the main walkway around the ballpark. Kate told her father they were going to explore a little and then followed Mike. She caught up to him at the top of the stairs. Mike had stopped in front of a food stand that was selling sugar-coated roasted almonds. He was watching as the woman at the stand mixed cinnamon and sugar with the warm nuts.

Mike took a long breath through his nose. "Smells like snickerdoodle cookies," he said when Kate arrived. "Maybe we should get some of these nuts so we have enough energy to chase the tiger."

"Um, Mike, we're not going to need that much energy," Kate said. "I'm not sure you know this, but stuffed tigers aren't real. If we found the tiger, I don't think it would run away from us."

Mike tapped his head with his finger. "I *know* that, Kate," he said. "But I thought we could try to figure out where the stuffed tiger *came* from. And that might lead us to the blackmailer."

Kate nodded. "Okay, good idea," she said. "Where do we start?"

"Let's walk around the park and check each souvenir shop for stuffed tigers." He pointed to the other side of the walkway. "You take the ones over there. I'll take the ones on this side."

For the next half hour, Mike and Kate circled the stadium. They checked one shop after another. They saw lots of Tigers bobbleheads, Tigers caps, Tigers baseball pillows, and even Tigers dog beds. But no stuffed tigers that matched the one they were looking for.

The closest they came was a stuffed panda with a big *D* on its chest and a large stuffed baseball with a tiger's face. The only stuffed tigers they found were small and cute, with googly eyes. The tigers wouldn't even be able to hold one baseball. At each new place, the salesperson pointed Mike or Kate to the googly-eyed tigers or the black and white stuffed pandas.

They had almost made it back to where they started when a huge cheer rose up from the crowd. Mike ran over to the railing and looked out at the field. It was the bottom of the fourth inning, and the Tigers had just scored a run!

"The Tigers are ahead by one now," Mike said as Kate joined him at the railing.

"I wish *we* were ahead by one tiger," Kate said. "Or maybe a hundred pandas."

Mike clenched his teeth and made a fist. He pretended to be mad. "If I see one more panda . . . ," he said.

Kate pushed Mike's fist down. "I know, I know," she said. "I kinda like the pandas. But maybe it's time to go to our seats and figure out where else we can look."

As they turned to head back, Mike spied a huge baseball floating in the air. And then another and another. They were all mounted on a big, spinning wheel over the nearby food court.

"Wow! A Ferris wheel!" Mike said. "Come on. Let's ride it. Maybe we can spot something new from the air!"

Mike and Kate ran across the walkway

to the end of the food court. At the end was a big Ferris wheel with a dozen cars shaped like giant baseballs! Each one was white with red stitching, and they had little doors and windows so riders could look out.

Mike and Kate waited in a short line while the operator loaded other fans into the baseball-shaped cars. When it was their turn, Mike hopped in first and slid across the plastic seat. Kate sat on the other side. As soon as the attendant closed the car's door, they were off. The car climbed high above the ballpark and rocked gently back and forth. Mike and Kate looked out the windows.

"This is amazing!" Mike said. "Look, you can see the street outside the ballpark. And over there are the food stands."

In the distance, Mike and Kate could hear fans clapping and cheering.

"Maybe Tony's coming up to bat," Kate said. "Too bad the stadium is in the way. Otherwise we could watch the game from here."

Mike's shoulders slumped. "I don't mind missing the game," he said. "I just wish we could find out who's threatening Tony."

Kate nodded. "I know. It feels like we're letting him down. When we're done, let's go check on Roger, since Tony said it might be him."

"Good idea," Mike said. "Maybe we can sneak into the clubhouse and check out his locker!"

As the Ferris wheel circled around, Mike and Kate watched the fans visiting the food stands below. After two more circles, Kate nudged Mike and pointed to a walkway on the upper level of the stadium. "Look, there's a souvenir shop that we missed," she said. "Let's check it out after the ride."

The Ferris wheel circled a few more times and then it stopped. Mike and Kate hopped off. They ran through the stadium and up the stairs to the souvenir shop they had spotted from the Ferris wheel. There was no line, so they both stepped right up to the counter and scanned the shelves. There were lots of orange T-shirts, blue baseball caps, bobbleheads, and even big orange foam claws. But no tigers.

An older woman with long brown hair leaned over the counter. "Can I help you?" she asked. "Looks like you have something specific in mind."

Kate nodded. "We do," she said. "We're looking for a stuffed tiger. It's orange and black and about this big." She motioned with her hands to show how wide and tall the tiger was. "Our friend has one, and we really like it. We've looked all over, but nobody has them."

The woman tapped her index finger on the counter. She had long red fingernails. "I know exactly what you're talking about," she said. "The tiger has a big smile and a Tigers baseball cap on?"

"Yes," Mike and Kate said together.

"Well, I'm sorry, but I don't have them, either," the saleswoman said.

Kate frowned. "You don't?" she asked. "Why not?"

"We had problems getting more of them, so the team stopped selling them," the woman said. "I had one left over from last year, but I just sold it a few weeks ago. How about one of these cute pandas instead?"

Kate tried not to laugh as Mike clenched his teeth. He took a breath and shook his head. "No thank you," he said. "We need the tiger." He and Kate turned to head back to their seats.

They had only taken a few steps when Kate turned around. "I just thought of something," she said. "Do you remember who bought the tiger?"

"Yes, I do," said the woman. "I don't know her name, but I'd recognize her because she works at the ballpark. She runs the hot dog stand near the merry-go-round."

A Furry Backpack

"Thanks!" Kate and Mike called. They wound their way through the crowds of fans toward the merry-go-round.

Halfway there, Mike stopped at a railing overlooking the field to check the score. "Yippee!" he said as he caught up to Kate. "It's the top of the seventh inning, and the Tigers are still ahead by one!"

When they reached the merry-go-round, the area was crowded with fans. Some waited in line for the ride. Others were at the condiment stations, squirting mustard or ketchup onto hot dogs.

Kate twirled around to check out the shops. Her long brown ponytail trailed out behind her head. "There it is," she said. She pointed to a hot dog stand on the other side of the food court. Five people were standing in line for hot dogs. She and Mike walked over.

It wasn't until they got close that the hot dog vendor turned around to hand a hot dog to the first person in line.

Mike grabbed Kate's arm. "Do you see who it is?" he asked.

"Yeah," Kate said. "It's Jane, the girl who told us about Tabby when we came in today."

Mike and Kate waited for the line to disappear and then stepped up to the counter. Jane looked at Mike and Kate and then glanced at Kate's L.A. Dodgers baseball hat. "Oh, hey, it's you guys again," she said. She pretended to swipe at them with her hand. "I hope you haven't been attacked by any other fearsome cats since you came in the park. There sure are a lot of them around here."

Kate smiled. "No, no more problems," she said. "But we were getting hungry."

Jane stepped back and motioned at all the food in the stand. "Well, you've come to the right place," she said. "What do you want? I've got it all."

Mike's eyes grew wide as they darted over all the options.

"How about some apple slices?" Jane asked.

"No," Mike said.

Jane held up a shiny blue bag. "Peanuts?" she asked.

Mike shook his head. "No."

Jane smiled. "Watch out," she said. "Three

strikes, and you're out! I'll give you one more choice. How about a hot dog?"

Mike tapped the counter. "Home run!" he said. "I'll take a hot dog with onions."

"Me too," Kate said.

Jane wrote down their orders in a notebook on the counter and used a calculator to figure out the cost. When she was done, she looked up and rolled her eyes. "The cash register's broken again," she said. "Now I have to do everything by hand and people have to wait. That's why this stand always has the longest line!"

Jane shook her head and then turned around to get the hot dogs. Mike and Kate checked over the stand. Hot dogs, onions, and peppers sizzled on a grill in the back corner. A tall soda machine with racks of red and white cups stood next to the grill. On the other side of the soda machine was a door that opened to the back of the stand. Mike and Kate could just see the field through the crack. Leaning against the frame of the door was a black backpack.

Mike nudged Kate. "Psst. Do you see what I see?" he whispered. He pointed to the backpack.

Kate's eyes grew wide. Just barely sticking out of the top of the backpack was a small tuft of striped fur!

Before Kate could respond, Jane plunked two hot dogs down on the counter. "Want anything else with that?" she asked.

"No thanks," Mike said. He handed over some cash, and Jane gave him his change. Mike tucked it in his pocket and pulled out his cell phone. "Mind if I take a picture for my website?" he asked. "I collect pictures of ballpark food stands."

"Sure, no problem," Jane said. She stood back and smiled.

Click! Click! Mike snapped a couple of pictures, and then slipped the phone back into his pocket. "Thanks," he said.

"But we did have a question," Kate said as she picked up her hot dog. "I'm looking to buy a stuffed tiger, like the one my friend has. But they don't sell them anymore. The woman at the souvenir shop told us she sold one to you recently. Do you want to sell it?"

Jane stopped cleaning up the counter. She paused like she was thinking. "Oh yeah," she said. "I did buy one a little while ago. But I gave it to my boyfriend. Sorry."

Kate smiled and shrugged. "No problem," she said. "Maybe we'll buy a panda instead."

Mike frowned and shook his head. "It's the Detroit *Tigers,* not the Detroit Pandas," he said. "We need a stuffed tiger." He picked up his hot dog and took a bite. "Thanks anyway."

As they munched on their hot dogs, Kate and Mike walked to a table in the center of the food court. When they were far enough away, Mike whispered to Kate, "Did you hear that? Jane said 'Three strikes, and you're out,' just like in Tony's note. And that sure looked like a stuffed tiger in the backpack to me."

"I think she was lying about the stuffed tiger!" Kate said.

"Me too," Mike said. He popped the last bit of hot dog in his mouth. "That's why I took the pictures."

"But how's a picture going to help?" Kate said.

"I'll explain later," Mike said. "Look, Jane's stand is getting busy again." A group of people had just lined up for food. Jane was busy filling more orders for hot dogs. "Follow me," he said.

Mike led Kate around to the back of Jane's stand. The door that they had spotted earlier was still slightly open. Mike put a finger to his lips, tiptoed over to the door, and peeked in. Through the small crack, he could see that

Jane was busy preparing hot dogs and waiting on fans.

Mike inched the door open just a bit more. Jane's black backpack rested against the door frame. There was definitely a piece of tiger fur poking out from its top. Not wasting any time, Mike reached out and opened the backpack's zipper partway. He tugged on the tuft of fur and lifted out the head of a stuffed tiger just like the one he and Kate had seen earlier!

Kate's hand flew to her mouth. Her eyes widened. She motioned for Mike to get out of there.

Mike pushed the tiger back down and zipped the backpack up. After he nudged the door closed, he and Kate scurried away from the stand.

When they were a safe distance away from Jane's stand, Kate let out a big breath. "Wow, I

don't believe it," she said. "She's got the tiger!"

Mike was so excited he was almost hopping up and down. "I know! I know!" he said. "Jane's the blackmailer! We've got to tell Tony."

A Strikeout

It was the bottom of the seventh inning, and the Tigers were still ahead by one run. The Tigers had just come off the field when Kate and Mike made their way down to the dugout.

As they approached the dugout, a security guard motioned for them to stop. "Sorry, but fans aren't allowed near here during games," she said.

"We're friends with Tony," Mike said. "He said we could ask for him."

The security guard studied Mike and

Kate. "Okay," she said. "Wait here and let me check." She disappeared into the dugout. A few moments later, Tony appeared.

"Hi, guys," he said. "I don't have long. What's up?"

"We found out who's writing those notes!" Mike said.

Tony's face lit up. "You did?" he asked. "Is it Roger?"

"No!" Kate said. "It's the girl who runs the hot dog stand near the merry-go-round." She explained how they tracked down the stuffed tiger and found it in Jane's backpack.

Tony gave Mike and Kate a high five. "Wow! That's great!" he growled. "Was the tiger filled with baseballs? Did you see the trophy?"

Mike scuffed the ground with his shoe. "Um," he said, "I'm not sure. I was worried about getting caught, so I didn't have time to

check if there were baseballs in the tiger. But it was the same *kind* of tiger."

Tony let out a sigh. "Ohhh . . . ," he said. "We need more proof. Lots of fans have those tigers.

Tell me who you think it is, and I'll have some-one check."

Mike pulled out his phone. "Here, look at the picture," he said. He pointed to the picture of Jane in the hot dog stand. "That's her. The backpack with the tiger is right here."

Tony took Mike's phone and studied the pic-ture for a minute. He let out a long, low whistle. And then he burst out laughing!

"You think Jane is blackmailing me?" Tony snorted. He shook his head. "Thanks for try-ing to help me, but I can promise you that Jane isn't the one doing it. I think you need to start over again."

"But it has to be her," Kate said. "We saw the stuffed tiger!"

"You saw *a* stuffed tiger," Tony said. "All the fans had them last year. And, more important, Jane's a great kid. She's worked for the Tigers for three years. They even put her in charge of the Dr. Tigers program, which helps kids at the children's hospital. She goes there every weekend to work with sick children."

One of the other players tapped Tony on the shoulder. The Mets were jogging off the field. Tony handed the phone to Mike. "Sorry, but I've got to get ready to bat," he said. "I doubt Jane's blackmailing me, but thanks for trying. Maybe you should start checking out Roger. I still think it might be him."

Tony hustled out to the on-deck circle to take some practice swings. Mike and Kate went back to their seats. Kate's father had filled five pages with notes on different players.

"I was wondering when you were going to return," he said. "Find anything out?"

Kate adjusted her baseball cap. Her brown ponytail stuck out through the hole in the back.

"No," she said. "Not really. Tony thinks it's Roger, the pitcher. But there's no way we can check him out during the game."

"Sorry," her dad said. He pointed to the field. The Tigers had a runner on first, and Tony was just stepping up to the plate. "At least it's a good game. They've got a chance to get a run or two here. Tony's been on a hitting streak lately."

The Mets pitcher's first ball blew right by Tony. He didn't even try to swing.

"STRIKE ONE!" called the umpire.

Tony stepped out of the batter's box and adjusted his batting gloves. He stared at the pitcher. Then he stepped back into the box and twisted his right foot in the dirt. Back and forth and back and forth it went. When he finally felt his foot was firmly planted, he held the bat high. The end of the barrel circled above his

shoulder like a buzzing bee. Tony looked ready.

The Detroit fans started to cheer and clap.

The pitcher threw again.

POP! The baseball popped into the catcher's mitt. It was a ball.

Tony took a few practice swings, then hoisted the bat over his shoulder again. The end of the bat drew small, fast circles in the air. Tony waited for the next pitch. The crowd was on its feet, cheering.

The pitcher threw the ball. Tony stepped forward with his left leg and dropped his shoulder. The bat swung around close to Tony's body. At the last second, he snapped his hands forward. *THWAP!*

The ball launched off Tony's bat. He dropped the bat and tore toward first base. The runner on first was already halfway to second base.

Mike and Kate jumped up with the rest of

the crowd and cheered. The ball kept climbing. It sailed over the outfield. The runners rounded the bases. The ball dropped into the bull pen behind the outfield fence.

It was a home run! The Tigers were now ahead by three.

The crowd went wild. Just as the first runner scored, a thundering *GRRROWL* came from the top of Detroit's scoreboard. Kate and Mike looked up just in time to see the eyes of the two tigers perched on top of the scoreboard light up bright red! They glowed as another loud *GRRROWL* echoed over the ballpark.

"Wow! That's so cool," Mike said. "The tigers growl when the *Tigers* hit a home run!"

After Tony crossed home plate, the crowd cheered one more time and sat down. Unfortunately, the next two batters struck out to end the inning. Between innings, Kate

leafed through the threatening notes again. Four of the paper scraps looked like they came from the same spiral-bound notebook. Each of them had the little cartoon tiger that Mike had pointed out earlier.

Kate showed the notes to Mike. "You thought we should look for a stuffed tiger," she said. "But maybe we should be looking for the notebook with the tigers in it instead. And I think I know where that notebook is!"

Kate tucked the notes into her pocket. She jumped out of her seat and bounded up the stairs just as Mike had done a few innings earlier. Mike followed as Kate wound her way through the stadium to the hot dog stand. Jane was still serving food. A few fans were waiting in line when Mike and Kate got there.

Kate took a place at the back of the line. "What are we doing?" Mike asked as he edged up beside her.

"You'll see," she said.

It didn't take too long to get to the front of the line. Jane had just finished wiping the counter when she looked up and noticed Mike and

Kate. "Still hungry?" she asked. "I've got lots more stuff you can try."

Kate shook her head. "No thanks," she said. "I just wanted to see if you had a piece of paper we could have. My cousin Mike wants to keep track of all the baseball players he's seeing, but he was too shy to ask."

Mike blushed.

Jane shrugged. "Sure," she said. She pulled the notebook on the counter closer to her and flipped it open to a blank page. Then she ripped out the sheet of paper and handed it to Mike. "Here you go," she said. "But feel free to come back when you get hungry!"

"Thanks! We will," Kate said as she and Mike turned and walked around the corner to the main walkway. Once they were out of sight of the hot dog stand, Kate grabbed Tony's pile of blackmail notes from her back pocket. She pulled out the notes that were written on note-book paper and placed the piece of paper they got from Jane on top. The new piece of paper had the same cartoon tiger on it that the other notes had.

"Look! They match *exactly*," Kate said. "Jane's got to be the blackmailer!"

A Golden Surprise

Mike took the papers from Kate and examined them. They really looked the same. "So it *is* her!" Mike said. "Just like we thought!"

He let out a sigh and handed the notes back to Kate. "But what if Tony *still* doesn't believe us? He really doesn't think Jane would do it."

Kate flipped her ponytail to the side of her head and started running her fingers through the strands of hair. "Maybe ... ," she said as she thought. After a minute, she gasped and snapped her fingers. "Maybe we don't need any more evidence to convince Tony!" she said.

"What do you mean?" Mike asked.

Kate gave Mike a big smile. "The best way to prove that Jane is the thief is to get her to lead us to the trophy!" she said.

Mike's eyes opened wide. "How would we do that?" he asked.

"Easy," Kate said. She pulled out a piece of paper and a pen from her pocket. Mike followed her to a table in the food court and watched as Kate wrote something on the paper and folded it in half. On the front Kate wrote JANE—IMPORTANT.

"What'd you write inside?" Mike asked. He tried to sneak a peek at the note. But Kate pulled it away from him. "You'll see!" she said. "Help me deliver this to Jane without her knowing."

Kate and Mike sneaked around to the other side of the hot dog stand. They stayed just to

the side of the stand, out of Jane's line of sight.
They waited until her customers were gone,
and then Kate crept closer.

When Jane turned around to check on the
hot dogs, Kate dashed up and slipped the note

on the counter. Then she and Mike ran to the
other side of the merry-go-round, where they
were hidden but could see Jane in the stand.
After a minute, she turned around and noticed
the note on the counter.

Jane picked it up and read it. A frown crossed her face, and she looked at the fans passing by like she was searching for someone. She checked her watch and then put a sign on the front counter. BE BACK IN 5 MINUTES, it read.

Kate pumped her fist. "She's falling for it!" she said.

Jane slipped her backpack on, went out the back door of the stand, and started walking down the hallway.

"Come on, we need to keep up," Kate said. She darted after Jane, taking care to stay hidden by the crowd so Jane wouldn't see her.

Mike dodged fans with hot dogs and sodas as he rushed to catch up to Kate. "Where's she going?" Mike asked as they trailed Jane.

Kate smiled. She tapped her head. "I thought the best way to catch a thief would be to act like one," she said.

Up ahead, Jane turned and hurried up a set of stairs to the upper level. Mike and Kate followed. At the top, Jane veered to the right.

"So what did the note say?" Mike asked.

"It said: *Are you missing something? We've found the trophy. If you want it back, leave the signed baseballs where the trophy is. Signed, Tony's Cubs,*" Kate said.

Mike rolled his eyes and held up his hands. "Are you crazy? *We. Don't. Have. The. Trophy!*" he said. "How is this going to work?"

Kate bared her teeth and growled softly at Mike. *"Grrrrrrr!"* she said. "I'm smart like a tiger. A tiger would know that when Jane read my note, she would get worried that someone was onto her. The first thing she'd do is check to see if the trophy really was missing. And by doing that, she'd lead us straight to it!"

A broad smile flashed across Mike's freckled

face. "Okay, that's a great idea," he admitted. "I *knew* there was a reason I let you hang around with me. . . ."

Mike and Kate continued to follow Jane. She made her way to a patio overlooking the main gate of the ballpark. It was filled with empty picnic tables. The area didn't look like it got a lot of use.

As Jane started to weave her way through the picnic tables, Mike and Kate ducked behind a trash can to watch. There was no other exit out of the picnic area. The trophy had to be nearby.

"Maybe she hid it under a picnic table," Mike said. "Or in that trash can over there."

"I don't know," Kate said. "I hope it's not in a trash can!" She studied the patio. A waist-high brick wall ran along the outside, overlooking the street below. In a front corner were the two

giant prowling tiger sculptures they had seen
from the street. Each of the tigers had two feet
on the brick wall and two feet on black metal
posts anchored into the patio floor.

Mike and Kate peeked around the edge of

the trash can. Jane headed straight for the tiger on the left. She slipped behind one of the picnic tables and knelt down by the tiger's rear feet.

Jane glanced around to make sure no one was watching, and then reached behind the big metal post that the tiger's feet were anchored to. A second later, she pulled out a gleaming gold trophy!

One Last Swipe

Mike and Kate rushed closer. Mike took out his phone.

Click! Click! Click! He snapped three pictures of Jane holding the trophy. "Want to hold it up so I can get a picture of that stolen trophy next to your face?" Mike asked.

Jane swung around. "Wh-wh-what are you doing here?" she asked.

Click! Click! Mike snapped a few more pictures.

"This isn't what it looks like," Jane said.

"Please, I can explain everything."

"You can explain it to Tony," Kate said. "We have all the evidence we need. We're going to show these pictures to him now. You want to come along and talk to him?"

Jane's shoulders slumped. She unzipped the backpack and slipped the trophy in it. "I can talk to Tony, but I've got to close the stand first," she said.

Mike and Kate followed Jane back to the hot dog stand. As she was closing up, a big roar rose from the crowd. Mike ran over to the railing overlooking the field. The Tigers had just won! The players were giving each other high fives and heading back to the dugout.

By the time Jane was finished, most of the fans had left. Mike and Kate led the way to the Tigers' dugout. On the way, they passed Kate's dad. He was still sitting in his seat making

notes. Kate waved for him to come over. He met them at the edge of the dugout and put away his notebook.

The security guards had shooed away the last of the fans who had been waiting nearby, hoping to get an autograph. The dugout was empty except for discarded paper cups and sunflower seed shells.

Kate walked over to one of the security guards. After she explained that they were there to see Tony, the security guard disappeared into the locker room. A few minutes later, Tony came out. He waved everyone into the dugout.

"Jane, what are you doing here?" Tony said.

Jane looked at the floor of the dugout and scuffed her feet on the concrete. She put the backpack down on the bench.

"We caught her red-handed," said Kate. She explained how they discovered that the notes were written on paper from Jane's notebook, and how they left a note for her and then followed her to the trophy.

When Kate was finished, Mike unzipped Jane's backpack. He dipped his hand in and pulled out the stuffed tiger. He felt the tiger's belly. Lump, lump, lump, lump, lump. The five baseballs *were* in there! Mike handed the tiger to Tony.

Tony felt the baseballs in the tiger and then shook his head. "I can't believe you were behind this, Jane," he said. "Just like Mike and Kate told me. Are you making extra money selling the autographed stuff?"

"No! I can explain. One of the sick kids at the hospital asked me to get an autograph from you," Jane said. "It meant a lot to him, but you're not signing things now. I thought if I held on to your trophy, I could get an autograph for him."

"But how'd you steal the trophy?" Kate asked.

Jane blushed. "I didn't exactly *steal* it," she said. "Tony left the trophy behind after a meeting. I think he forgot to put it back in his bag. I picked it up and went to look for him, but he had already left. I was just going to give it back to Tony the next time I saw him. But then I figured out I could use it to get autographs for the kids. I guess I got carried away."

"What did you do with all the stuff that Tony autographed?" Mike asked.

"I gave it to the kids at the hospital," Jane said. "They're huge fans of Tony's. You wouldn't believe how much it meant to them that he was signing things for them. I know I should have stopped, but I just couldn't. I figured a few baseballs, shirts, and other stuff wouldn't mean that much to the Tigers."

"You should have just come to me," Tony said.

"But I know the coach won't let you sign autographs now," Jane said. "That's why I had to do it this way. All the kids at the hospital want Tony the Tiger's autograph. I was just trying to get it for them."

Tony hung his head for a moment. "You meant well," he said, looking up. "But taking my trophy and blackmailing me is still wrong, even if you're doing it for a good reason."

Jane nodded. "I know," she said. "I'm sorry."

"What about the trophy?" Tony asked. "I need that back."

Mike reached into the backpack again. This time he pulled out the shiny gold trophy. It had a baseball player hitting a baseball on top. The black base of the trophy had a big brass plate with writing on it.

"My missing Little League trophy!" Tony said. "That's great!"

Tony tried to reach for the trophy, but Mike took a step back and read the writing on it. When he was finished, he burst out laughing. "No wonder you didn't want anyone on the team to see this!" Mike said.

He handed the trophy to Kate. She read the words on the brass plate out loud. *"East City Little League MVP—Tony 'Baloney' Maloney."*

"Tony Baloney?" Mike asked. "Your nickname was really Tony Baloney?"

Tony sighed. "It was. That trophy's my good-luck charm," he said. "But if the guys on the team saw it, they'd start calling me Tony Baloney. That's why I took the trophy with me to the meeting. My locker was being cleaned, so I wanted to keep it close to me, but then I lost it."

Tony picked up the trophy. "I loved playing Little League. But I sure didn't like that nickname."

Tony bared his teeth and let out a loud *ROAR!* "Now I'm Tony the Tiger!" he growled.

Mike, Kate, and Mr. Hopkins laughed.

"Thanks to you two, I can be Tony the Tiger once again!" he said. "If you still have the baseball card, Mike, I'd be happy to sign it."

"Sure! That would be great," Mike said. He pulled the card out of his pocket and handed it to Tony. Tony found a pen in the back of the dugout and started to sign the baseball card for Mike.

"Wait!" Kate said. "I thought you weren't supposed to sign things."

Tony smiled. He held the pen up with his left hand and wiggled it. "I'm not," he said. "But I've been practicing at home, and I've learned how to write with my *left* hand, so there's no problem now!"

Tony finished signing and handed the card back. Mike read the message out loud: *To Mike and Kate, the two fiercest tiger cubs I know!* *—Tony the Tiger*

"Thanks, Tony!" Kate said. "I'm glad we found your trophy."

"So am I," Tony said. He turned to Jane. She was slumped on the bench. "I'm going to have to tell your manager about what you did."

"Please don't have me fired," Jane said. "I love working for the Tigers. I know I made a big mistake."

Tony picked up his trophy and studied it. "As long as I have this back, I guess it's not a big problem," he said. "But if you want to put this behind you, you'll have to do something for me."

Jane looked up. "I'll do anything to make this right," she said.

"Then go buy thirty baseballs and meet me at the front gate tomorrow morning at ten o'clock," Tony said. "You're going to take me to visit your friends in the hospital. Now that I can write with my left hand, I'll be able to sign all the balls they want."

Jane jumped up. She gave Tony a hug. "Thank you!" she said. "The kids will be thrilled. And I'll never do anything like this again. I'm going to go get those baseballs. I'll see you tomorrow morning."

Mike, Kate, and Mr. Hopkins followed Tony out of the dugout. Just as Kate left the dugout, an orange and white paw swiped down in front of her. She gasped and tried to jump out of the way. But she wasn't fast enough. The paw sent Kate's blue L.A. Dodgers baseball cap flying! It landed upside down on the field.

Kate jumped forward and looked up. It was Tabby, the cat from the ballpark entrance. Kate shook her head and picked up her hat. "I guess I have to be a lot more careful around these tigers," she said. "They're fierce!"

"Or maybe you just need to follow me," Tony said. He walked over to the edge of the dugout and picked up the cat. Tabby nestled snugly in his broad arms while he petted her. "I think Tabby is saying that it's time for me to buy you both some brand-new Detroit Tigers baseball hats!"

Dugout Notes
☆ The Detroit ☆
Tigers' Ballpark

Liquid fireworks. When Detroit hits a home run, the fountain above the center-field wall erupts in time to music. Colored lights make the sprays of water appear different colors. The team calls it a liquid fireworks display!

Tiger, tiger, burning bright. The tiger heads on the outside of Detroit's stadium are clutching baseballs in their teeth. But the best thing about the tigers is that the baseballs light up at night!

Motor City. Detroit is known as Motor City because lots of car companies were started there. In the early 1900s, Henry Ford started the Ford Motor Company. He figured out how to make his cars for less money, so more people could buy them. The Model T Ford became the most popular car in America.

Baseball carnival. As Mike and Kate found out, the Tigers' stadium has both a Ferris wheel and a merry-go-round inside it. The Ferris wheel has baseball-shaped cars and is fifty feet tall. Riders can choose from one of thirty tigers or two chariots on the merry-go-round!

Shiny statues. There are six shiny steel statues of famous Detroit Tigers players near the center-field wall. They're made in a special way to show the players in action. The play-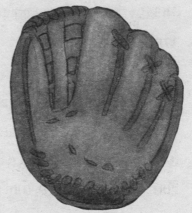ers are Ty Cobb, Charlie Gehringer, Hank Greenberg, Willie Horton, Al Kaline, and Hal Newhouser.

World Series winners. The Tigers have won four World Series titles: 1935, 1945, 1968, and 1984.

An old team. The Detroit Tigers are one of the American League's eight original teams. They started in 1894. They're the oldest baseball team in the American League to stay in the same city with the same name.

A terrific name. History is murky on how the Tigers got their name, but there are legends. One says it was because of the orange stripes on the players' black stockings. Another says it was because a sportswriter compared the team to a college team, the Princeton Tigers. Still another says they were named after a Civil War military unit from Detroit that was called the Tigers.

Ty Cobb. Ty Cobb was a mean and nasty Tiger. But he was also one of the best baseball players of all time. He played for the Detroit Tigers for twenty-one years, from 1905 to 1926. Although he stopped playing close to one hundred years ago, he still holds some baseball records!

Don't miss a single
Ballpark Mystery®!

The Rookie Blue Jay

Mike and Kate can't wait to watch their rookie hero Dusty Martin in action. But something is throwing the Blue Jays' star off his game. Then, when no one else is looking, Mike sees mysterious ghost lights flying across the field. Is the ballpark haunted? Could Dusty have seen the lights, too?

BATTER UP AND CRACK THE CASE!

BALLPARK® Mysteries

BASEBALL SLEUTHING FUN
WITH MORE TO COME!

RandomHouseKids.com

Get ready for more baseball adventure!

Did Babe Ruth curse the Boston Red Sox
when he moved to the New York Yankees?

Available now!